The Art Show

by Susan McCloskey
illustrated by Gary Bialke

Scott Foresman

Editorial Offices: Glenview, Illinois • New York, New York
Sales Offices: Reading, Massachusetts • Duluth, Georgia
Glenview, Illinois • Carrollton, Texas • Menlo Park, California

"Oh! Fiddle!" said Miles
Crocodile. "The art show is
tomorrow! I forgot all about it!"

Miles did not know what to make for the show.

"Maybe I'll make a big, round basket," he said. "Or a soap dinosaur. Or a painting."

"Yes!" said Miles. "A painting!"

So Miles got busy.

After a while, Miles stood back.
He liked it!
    "There!" he said. "It's done.
Finished!"

But the wind had other ideas.
It picked up the painting and
blew it outside.

It dropped it into a big round
puddle. Then it picked up the
painting again.

It dropped the painting in the
woods. Then it picked it up again.

It dropped the painting beside a
round pond. But it was not finished
yet. It picked up the painting again.

Miles looked and looked. He
could not find his lost painting.

Poor Miles! The next day he
cried all the way to the art show.
He had never cried so hard.

When he got there, Miles met his
friend Beth.

"Great work, Miles!" Beth said.
"It's so good!"

Ted said, "I love it!"
Brad said, "It looks great!"
Tina said, "I wish I could
paint like that!"
Miles said, "What?"

"Your painting!" said Tina.
"I found it outside where you
left it. There it is!"

There was Miles's painting.
Or was it the wind's? Anyway,
it did not win a blue ribbon. But
Miles was proud that his friends
liked it. So he did not even care!